a window cleaner

a guinea pig

Using this book

Ladybird's *talkabouts* are ideal for encouraging children
to talk about what they see. Bold colourful pictures
and simple questions help to develop early learning
skills – such as matching, counting and
detailed observation.

Look at this book with your child. First talk about the
pictures yourself, and point out things to look at. Let
your child take her* time. With encouragement, she
will start to join in, talking about the familiar things in
the pictures. Help her to count objects, to look for
things that match, and to talk about what is going on
in the picture stories.

To avoid the clumsy use of he/she, the child is referred to as 'she',
talkabouts *are suitable for both boys and girls.*

Published by Ladybird Books Ltd
80 Strand London WC2R ORL
A Penguin Company

1 3 5 7 9 10 8 6 4 2

© LADYBIRD BOOKS MMIII

Printed in Italy

Here are some families.
Talk about what they are doing.

People I like

written by Lorraine Horsley
illustrated by Alex Ayliffe

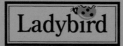
Ladybird

Who is in your family?

This granny and grandad have
brought Millie to the park.
Tell the story.

Lots of people come to Jane's house.

What jobs do they do?

Can you match these things to the people?

Mrs Vee is a vet. She looks after people's pets when they are ill.

Who do these pets belong to?

How many...

budgies?

puppies?

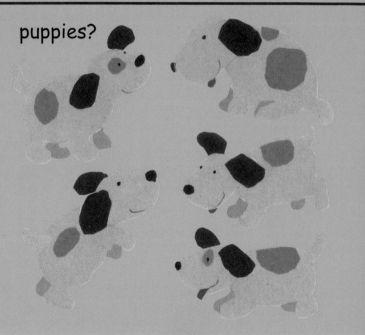

fish?

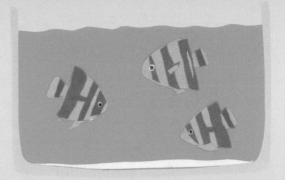

kittens?

guinea pigs?

Which pet would you choose?

Mr Henry is a hairdresser.
He cuts hair.
Tell the story.

Can you match these things to their shadows?

Mrs Loop is a librarian.
She stamps the books so they can
be taken out of the library.

Do you know these stories?
What is your favourite story?

Mrs Prince is the playgroup leader.
She's helping to paint a picture.
What are the other children doing?

25

Say the names of these colours.

red

blue

yellow

orange

pink

Which colours have been used to paint the picture?

purple

white

brown

green

black

Mr Dot is a doctor. He helps children to get better when they are ill.

Can you match these things to their shadow?

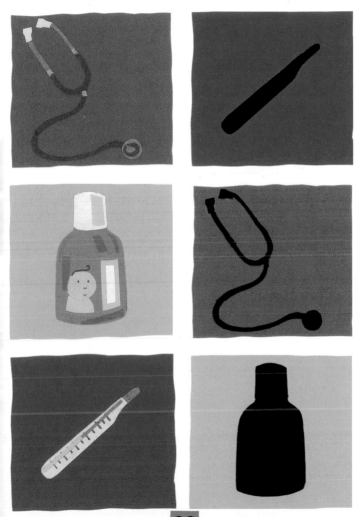

Can you find these as well?

a dog

a hairbrush

a fireman